A NOTE TO PARENTS

Reading is often considered the most important skill children learn in primary grades. Much can be done at home to lay the foundation for early reading success.

When they read, children use the following to figure out words: story and picture clues, how a word is used in a sentence, and sound/spelling relationships. The **Hello Reader!** *Phonics Fun* series focuses on sound/spelling relationships through phonics activities. Phonics instruction unlocks the door to understanding sounds and the letters or spelling patterns that represent them.

The **Hello Reader!** *Phonics Fun* series is divided into the following three sets of books, based on important phonic elements:

- **Sci-Fi Phonics**: word families
- **Monster Phonics**: consonants, blends, and digraphs
- **Funny Tale Phonics**: short and long vowels

Learn About Consonants

The Monster Phonics stories, including *Monster Town Fair*, feature words that begin with the same sound. These books help children become aware of and use consonant sounds when decoding, or sounding out, new words. After reading the book, you might wish to begin lists of words that begin with the same sound. Your child can use these lists for reading practice or as reference when spelling words.

Enjoy the Activities

- Challenge your child to build words using the letters and word parts provided. Help your child by demonstrating how to sound out new words.
- Match words with pictures to help your child attach meaning to text.
- Become word detectives by identifying story words with the same sound, letter, or spelling pattern.
- Keep the activities game-like and praise your child's efforts.

Develop Fluency

Encourage your child to read these books again and again and again. Each time, set a different purpose for reading.

- Look for rhyming words or words that begin and end with the same sound.
- Suggest to your child that he or she read the book to a friend, family member, or even a pet.

Whatever you do, have fun with the books and instill the joy of reading in your child. It is one of the most important things you can do!

— Wiley Blevins, Reading Specialist
Ed.M., Harvard University

To my most beautiful Gwen
—J.B.S.

For Margaret Lindsay,
my extraordinary high school art teacher
—N.E.

Text copyright © 1998 by Judith Bauer Stamper.
Illustrations copyright © 1998 by Nate Evans.
All rights reserved. Published by Scholastic Inc.
HELLO READER! and CARTWHEEL BOOKS and associated logos
are trademarks and/or registered trademarks of Scholastic Inc.

Library of Congress Cataloging-in-Publication Data

Stamper, Judith Bauer.
    Monster Town fair/ by Judith Bauer Stamper; illustrated by Nate Evans;
    phonics activities by Wiley Blevins.
       p.   cm.—(Hello reader! Phonics fun. Monster phonics)
    "Consonants: r, b, f, c."
    "Cartwheel Books."
    Summary: Little Monster visits the Monster Town fair, where he is
introduced to a new letter of the alphabet at every turn. Includes related
phonics activities.
    ISBN 0-590-76268-0
    [1. Monsters—Fiction. 2. Fairs—Fiction. 3. Alphabet.]
I. Evans, Nate, ill. II. Blevins, Wiley. III. Title. IV. Series.
PZ7.S78612Mo   1998
[E]—dc21
                                                    97-23399
                                                      CIP
                                                      AC

10 9 8 7 6 5 4   8 9/9 0/0 01 02

Printed in the U.S.A.   24
First printing, March 1998

Monster Town Fair

by Judith Bauer Stamper
Illustrated by Nate Evans
Phonics Activities by Wiley Blevins

Hello Reader! Phonics Fun
Monster Phonics • Consonants: *r, b, f, c*

SCHOLASTIC INC. Cartwheel BOOKS®

New York Toronto London Auckland Sydney

Come to the fair
in Monster Town.
Follow the funny
monster clown.

The fair has letter games and fun.

Grab a balloon
and run, run, run!

Today is R day at the fair.

Look for R words everywhere.

Ride on a robot.
See a rock 'n' roll show.

Fly a red rocket
over the rainbow.

Today is B day at the fair.

Look for B words everywhere.

Go up in a balloon.
Win a bear with a ball.

Ride bikes and boats
and that's not all!

Today is F day
at the fair.

Fly on a fish.
Hop on a frog.

Fortune-teller

F

5

Get a fright from
five faces in a fog!

Today is C day
at the fair.

Look for C words
everywhere.

C-C-CLICK

See wild cats in cages.
Ride a camel up and down.

Crawl through a creepy cave
after the clown.

Find more letter fun everywhere.

See all the letters . . .

at the Monster Town Fair!

• PHONICS ACTIVITIES •
Letter Cards

Use the letters on the cards to make a word that names each picture.

Which Belong?

Point to the pictures that belong in each tent. Each tent's pictures must begin with the same sound.

Build a Word

Add the letter in the monster's hat to the word endings below.

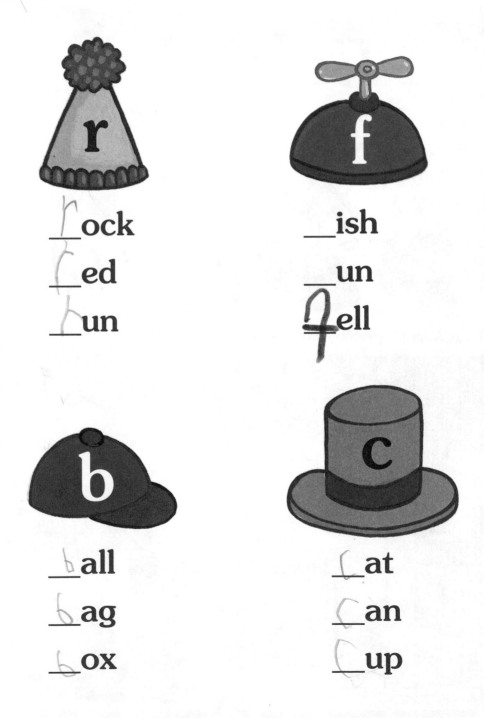

r
_r_ock
_r_ed
_r_un

f
__ish
__un
_f_ell

b
_b_all
_b_ag
_b_ox

c
_c_at
_c_an
_c_up

Picture Match
Find the word in the story that names each picture.

Answers

Letter Cards

fan
can
cat
bat
rat

Which Belong?

Build a Word

rock	fish
red	fun
run	fell
ball	cat
bag	can
box	cup

Picture Match

ball	five
bear	camel
fish	robot